The Poems of Schiller Suppressed Period

FRIEDRICH SCHILLER

Published in 1851

TABLE OF CONTENTS

THE JOURNALISTS AND MINOS
BACCHUS IN THE PILLORY
SPINOSA
TO THE FATES
THE PARALLEL
KLOPSTOCK AND WIELAND
THE MUSES' REVENGE
THE HYPOCHONDRIACAL PLUTO
REPROACH TO LAURA
THE SIMPLE PEASANT
ACTAEON
MAN'S DIGNITY
THE MESSIAD
THOUGHTS ON THE 1ST OCTOBER 1781
EPITAPH
QUIRL
THE PLAGUE
MONUMENT OF MOOR THE ROBBER
THE BAD MONARCHS
THE SATYR AND MY MUSE
THE PEASANTS
THE WINTER NIGHT
THE WIRTEMBERGER
THE MOLE
HYMN TO THE ETERNAL
DIALOGUE
ON A CERTAIN PHYSIOGNOMIST
TRUST IN IMMORTALITY
APPENDIX OF POEMS ETC. IN SCHILLER'S
DRAMATIC WORKS
FOOTNOTES

FRIEDRICH SCHILLER

THE JOURNALISTS AND MINOS

I chanced the other eve,
But how I ne'er will tell,
The paper to receive.
That's published down in hell.

In general one may guess,
I little care to see
This free-corps of the press
Got up so easily;

But suddenly my eyes
A side-note chanced to meet,
And fancy my surprise
At reading in the sheet:

"For twenty weary springs"
(The post from Erebus,
Remark me, always brings
Unpleasant news to us)

"Through want of water, we
Have well-nigh lost our breath;
In great perplexity
Hell came and asked for Death;

"'They can wade through the Styx,
Catch crabs in Lethe's flood;
Old Charon's in a fix,
His boat lies in the mud,

"'The dead leap over there,
The young and old as well;
The boatman gets no fare,
And loudly curses hell.'

"King Minos bade his spies
In all directions go;
The devils needs must rise,
And bring him news below.

"Hurrah! The secret's told
They've caught the robber's nest;
A merry feast let's hold!
Come, hell, and join the rest!

"An author's countless band,
Stalked round Cocytus' brink,
Each bearing in his hand
A glass for holding ink.

"And into casks they drew
The water, strange to say,
As boys suck sweet wine through
An elder-reed in play.

"Quick! o'er them cast the net,
Ere they have time to flee!
Warm welcome ye will get,
So come to Sans-souci!

"Smelt by the king ere long,
He sharpened up his tooth,
And thus addressed the throng
(Full angrily, in truth):

"'The robbers is't we see?
What trade? What land, perchance?'—
'German news-writers we!'—

Enough to make us dance!

"'A wish I long have known
To bid ye stop and dine,
Ere ye by Death were mown,
That brother-in-law of mine.

"'Yet now by Styx I swear,
Whose flood ye would imbibe,
That torments and despair
Shall fill your vermin-tribe!

"'The pitcher seeks the well,
Till broken 'tis one day;
They who for ink would smell,
The penalty must pay.

"'So seize them by their thumbs,
And loosen straight my beast
E'en now he licks his gums,
Impatient for the feast.'—

"How quivered every limb
Beneath the bull-dog's jaws
Their honors baited him,
And he allowed no pause.

"Convulsively they swear,
Still writhe the rabble rout,
Engaged with anxious care
In pumping Lethe out."

Ye Christians, good and meek,
This vision bear in mind;
If journalists ye seek,
Attempt their thumbs to find.

Defects they often hide,
As folks whose hairs are gone
We see with wigs supplied
Probatum! I have done!

FRIEDRICH SCHILLER

BACCHUS IN THE PILLORY

Twirl him! twirl him! blind and dumb
Deaf and dumb,
Twirl the cane so troublesome!
Sprigs of fashion by the dozen
Thou dost bring to book, good cousin.
Cousin, thou art not in clover;
Many a head that's filled with smoke
Thou hast twirled and well-nigh broke,
Many a clever one perplexed,
Many a stomach sorely vexed,
Turning it completely over;
Many a hat put on awry,
Many a lamb chased cruelly,
Made streets, houses, edges, trees,
Dance around us fools with ease.
Therefore thou are not in clover,
Therefore thou, like other folk,
Hast thy head filled full of smoke,
Therefore thou, too, art perplexed,
And thy stomach's sorely vexed,
For 'tis turned completely over;
Therefore thou art not in clover.

Twirl him! twirl him! blind and dumb
Deaf and dumb,
Twirl the carle so troublesome!
Seest thou how our tongues and wits
Thou hast shivered into bits—

Seest thou this, licentious wight?
How we're fastened to a string,
Whirled around in giddy ring,
Making all like night appear,
Filling with strange sounds our ear?
Learn it in the stocks aright!
When our ears wild noises shook,
On the sky we cast no look,
Neither stock nor stone reviewed,
But were punished as we stood.
Seest thou now, licentious wight?
That, to us, yon flaring sun
Is the Heidelbergers' tun;
Castles, mountains, trees, and towers,
Seem like chopin-cups of ours.
Learn'st thou now, licentious wight?
Learn it in the stocks aright!

Twirl him! twirl him! blind and dumb,
Deaf and dumb,
Twirl the carle so troublesome!
Kinsman, once so full of glee,
Kinsman, where's thy drollery,
Where thy tricks, thou cunning one?
All thy tricks are spent and past,
To the devil gone at last
Like a silly fop thou'lt prate,
Like a washerwoman rate.
Thou art but a simpleton.
Now thou mayest—more shame to thee—
Run away, because of me;
Cupid, that young rogue, may glory
Learning wisdom from thy story;
Haste, thou sluggard, hence to flee
As from glass is cut our wit,
So, like lightning, 'twill be split;
If thou won't be chased away,
Let each folly also stay
Seest my meaning? Think of me!
Idle one, away with thee!

SPINOSA

A mighty oak here ruined lies,
Its top was wont to kiss the skies,
Why is it now o'erthrown?—
The peasants needed, so they said,
Its wood wherewith to build a shed,
And so they've cut it down.

TO THE FATES

Not in the crowd of masqueraders gay,
Where coxcombs' wit with wondrous splendor flares,
And, easier than the Indian's net the prey,
The virtue of young beauties snares;—

Not at the toilet-table of the fair,
Where vanity, as if before an idol, bows,
And often breathes a warmer prayer
Than when to heaven it pays its vows;

And not behind the curtain's cunning veil,
Where the world's eye is hid by cheating night,
And glowing flames the hearts assail,
That seemed but chilly in the light,—

Where wisdom we surprise with shame-dyed lip,
While Phoebus' rays she boldly drinks,
Where men, like thievish children, nectar sip,
And from the spheres e'en Plato sinks—

To ye—to ye, O lonely sister-band,
Daughters of destiny, ascend,
When o'er the lyre all-gently sweeps my hand,
These strains, where bliss and sadness blend.

You only has no sonnet ever wooed,
To win your gold no usurer e'er sighed

No coxcomb e'er with plaints your steps pursued,
For you, Arcadian shepherd ne'er has died.

Your gentle fingers ye forever ply,
Life's nervous thread with care to twist,
Till sound the clanging shears, and fruitlessly
The tender web would then resist.

Since thou my thread of life hast kindly spun,
Thy hand, O Clotho, I now kiss!
Since thou hast spared that life whilst scarce begun,
Receive this nosegay, Lachesis!

Full often thorns upon the thread,
But oftener roses, thou hast strung;
For thorns and roses there outspread,
Clotho, to thee this lay be sung!

Oft did tempestuous passions rise,
And threat to break the thread by force;
Oft projects of gigantic size
Have checked its free, unfettered course.

Oft, in sweet hours of heavenly bliss,
Too fine appeared the thread to me;
Still oftener, when near sorrow's dark abyss,
Too firm its fabric seemed to be.

Clotho, for this and other lies,
Thy pardon I with tears implore;
Henceforth I'll take whatever prize
Sage Clotho gives, and asks no more.

But never let the shears cut off a rose—
Only the thorns,—yet as thou will'st!
Let, if thou will'st, the death-shears, sharply close,
If thou this single prayer fulfill'st!

Oh, goddess! when, enchained to Laura's breath,
My spirit from its shell breaks free,
Betraying when, upon the gates of death,
My youthful life hangs giddily,

Let to infinity the thread extend,
'Twill wander through the realms of bliss,—
Then, goddess, let thy cruel shears descend!
Then let them fall, O Lachesis!

THE PARALLEL

Her likeness Madame Ramler bids me find;
I try to think in vain, to whom or how
Beneath the moon there's nothing of the kind.—
I'll show she's like the moon, I vow!

The moon—she rouges, steals the sun's bright light,
By eating stolen bread her living gets,—
Is also wont to paint her cheeks at night,
While, with untiring ardor, she coquets.

The moon—for this may Herod give her thanks!—
Reserves her best till night may have returned;
Our lady swallows up by day the francs
That she at night-time may have earned.

The moon first swells, and then is once more lean,
As surely as the month comes round;
With Madame Ramler 'tis the same, I ween—
But she to need more time is found!

The moon to love her silver-horns is said,
But makes a sorry show;
She likes them on her husband's head,—
She's right to have it so

FRIEDRICH SCHILLER

KLOPSTOCK AND WIELAND

(WHEN THEIR MINIATURES WERE HANGING SIDE BY SIDE.)

In truth, when I have crossed dark Lethe's river,
The man upon the right I'll love forever,
For 'twas he first that wrote for me.
For all the world the left man wrote, full clearly,
And so we all should love him dearly;
Come, left man! I must needs kiss thee!

THE MUSES' REVENGE

An Anecdote Of Helicon.

Once the nine all weeping came
To the god of song
"Oh, papa!" they there exclaim—
"Hear our tale of wrong!

"Young ink-lickers swarm about
Our dear Helicon;
There they fight, manoeuvre, shout,
Even to thy throne.

"On their steeds they galop hard
To the spring to drink,
Each one calls himself a bard—
Minstrels—only think!

"There they—how the thing to name!
Would our persons treat—
This, without a blush of shame,
We can ne'er repeat;

"One, in front of all, then cries,
'I the army lead!'
Both his fists he wildly plies,
Like a bear indeed!

"Others wakes he in a trice
With his whistlings rude;
But none follow, though he twice
Has those sounds renewed.

"He'll return, he threats, ere long,
And he'll come no doubt!
Father, friend to lyric song,
Please to show him out!"

Father Phoebus laughing hears
The complaint they've brought;
"Don't be frightened, pray, my dears,
We'll soon cut them short!

"One must hasten to hell-fire,
Go, Melpomene!
Let a fury borrow lyre,
Notes, and dress, of thee.

"Let her meet, in this array,
One of these vile crews,
As though she had lost her way,
Soon as night ensues.

"Then with kisses dark, I trust,
They'll the dear child greet,
Satisfying their wild lust
Just as it is meet!"—

Said and done!—Then one from hell
Soon was dressed aright.
Scarcely had the prey, they tell,
Caught the fellow's sight,

Than, as kites a pigeon follow,
They attacked her straight—
Part, not all, though, I can swallow
Of what folks relate.

If fair boys were 'mongst the band,
How came they to be—
This I cannot understand,—

In such company?

The goddess a miscarriage had, good lack!
And was delivered of an—Almanac!

THE HYPOCHONDRIACAL PLUTO

A ROMANCE.

BOOK I.

The sullen mayor who reigns in hell,
By mortals Pluto hight,
Who thrashes all his subjects well,
Both morn and eve, as stories tell,
And rules the realms of night,
All pleasure lost in cursing once,
All joy in flogging, for the nonce.

The sedentary life he led
Upon his brazen chair
Made his hindquarters very red,
While pricks, as from a nettle-bed,
He felt both here and there:
A burning sun, too, chanced to shine,
And boiled down all his blood to brine.

'Tis true he drank full many a draught
Of Phlegethon's black flood;
By cupping, leeches, doctor's craft,
And venesection, fore and aft,
They took from him much blood.
Full many a clyster was applied,
And purging, too, was also tried.

27

His doctor, versed in sciences,
With wig beneath his hat,
Argued and showed with wondrous ease,
From Celsus and Hippocrates,
When he in judgment sat,—
"Right worshipful the mayor of hell,
The liver's wrong, I see full well."

"He's but a booby," Pluto said,
"With all his trash and pills!
A man like me—pray where's his head?
A young man yet—his wits have fled!
While youth my veins yet fills!
Unless electuaries he'll bring,
Full in his face my club I'll fling!"

Or right or wrong,—'twas a hard case
To weather such a trial;
(Poor men, who lose a king's good grace!)
He's straight saluted in the face
By every splint and phial.
He very wisely made no fuss;
This hint he learnt of Cerberus.

"Go! fetch the barber of the skies,
Apollo, to me soon!"
An airy courier straightway flies
Upon his beast, and onward hies,
And skims past poles and moon;
As he went off, the clock struck four,
At five his charger reached the door.

Just then Apollo happened—"Heigh-ho!
A sonnet to have made?"
Oh, dear me, no!—upon Miss Io
(Such is the tale I heard from Clio)
The midwife to have played.
The boy, as if stamped out of wax,
Might Zeus as father fairly tax.

He read the letter half asleep,
Then started in dismay:

"The road is long, and hell is deep,
Your rocks I know are rough and steep . . .
Yet like a king he'll pay!"
He dons his cap of mist and furs,
Then through the air the charger spurs.

With locks all frizzled a la mode,
And ruffles smooth and nice,
In gala dress, that brightly glowed
(A gift Aurora had bestowed),
With watch-chains of high price,
With toes turned out, and chapeau bas,
He stood before hell's mighty czar.

BOOK II.

The grumbler, in his usual tone,
Received him with a curse:
"To Pomerania straight begone!
Ugh! how he smells of eau de Cologne!
Why, brimstone isn't worse.
He'd best be off to heaven again,
Or he'll infect hell's wide domain."

The god of pills, in sore surprise,
A spring then backwards took:
"Is this his highness' usual guise?
'Tis in the brain, I see, that lies
The mischief—what a look!
See how his eyes in frenzy roll!
The case is bad, upon my soul!

"A journey to Elysium
The infectus would dissolve,
Making the saps less tough become,
As through the Capitolium
And stomach they revolve.
Provisionally be it so:
Let's start then—but incognito!"

"Ay, worthy sir, no doubt well meant!
If, in these regions hazy,
As with you folk, so charged with scent,

You dapper ones who heaven frequent,
'Twere proper to be lazy,
If hell a master needed not,
Why, then I'd follow on the spot!

"Ha! if the cat once turned her back,
Pray where would be the mice?
They'd sally forth from every crack,
My very mufti would attack,
Spoil all things in a trice!
Oddsbodikins! 'tis pretty cool!
I'll let him see I'm no such fool!

"A pleasant uproar happened erst,
When they assailed my tower!
No fault of mine 'twas, at the worst,
That from their desks and chains to burst
Philosophers had power.
What, has there e'er escaped a poet?
Help, heaven! what misery to know it!

"When days are long, folks talk more stuff!
Upon your seats, no doubt,
With all your cards and music rough,
And scribblings too, 'tis hard enough
The moments to eke out.
Idleness, like a flea will gnaw
On velvet cushions,—as on straw.

"My brother no attempt omits
To drive away ennui;
His lightning round about him flits,
The target with his storms he hits
(Those howls prove that to me),
Till Rhea's trembling shoulders ache,
And force me e'en for hell to quake.

"Were I grandfather Coelus, though,
You wouldn't soon escape!
Into my belly straight you'd go,
And in your swaddling-clothes cry 'oh!'
And through five windows gape!
First o'er my stream you'd have to come,

And then, perhaps, to Elysium!

"Your steed you mounted, I dare say,
In hopes to catch a goose;
If it is worth the trouble, pray
Tell what you've heard from me to-day,
At shaving time, to Zeus.
Just leave him then to swallow it;
I don't care what he thinks a bit;

"You'd better now go homeward straight!
Your servant! there's the door!
For all your pains—one moment wait!
I'll give you—liberal is the rate—
A piece of ruby-ore.
In heaven such things are rareties;
We use them for base purposes."

BOOK III.

The god at once, then, said farewell,
At small politeness striving;
When sudden through the crowds of hell
A flying courier rushed pell-mell,
From Tellus' bounds arriving.
"Monarch! a doctor follows me!
Behold this wondrous prodigy!"

"Place for the doctor!" each one said—
He comes with spurs and whip,
To every one he nods his head,
As if he had been born and bred
In Tartarus—the rip!
As jaunty, fearless, full of nous
As Britons in the Lower House.

"Good morrow, worthy sirs!—Ahem!
I'm glad to see that here
(Where all they of Prometheus' stem
Must come, whene'er the Fates condemn)
One meets with such good cheer!
Why for Elysium care a rush?
I'd rather see hell's fountains gush!"

31

"Stop! stop! his impudence, I vow,
Its due reward shall meet;
By Charles's wain, I swear it now!
He must—no questions I'll allow,—
Prescribe me a receipt.
All hell is mine, I'm Pluto hight!
Make haste to bring your wares to light!"

The doctor, with a knowing look,
The swarthy king surveyed;
He neither felt his pulse, nor took
The usual steps,—(see Galen's book),—
No difference 'twould have made
As piercing as electric fire
He eyed him to his heart's desire.

"Monarch! I'll tell thee in a trice
The thing that's needed here;
Though desperate may seem the advice—
The case itself is very nice—
And children dragons fear.
Devil must devil eat!—no more!—
Either a wife,—or hellebore!

"Whether she scold, or sportive play,
('Tween these, no medium's known),
She'll drive the incubus away
That has assailed thee many a day
Upon thine iron throne.
She'll make the nimble spirits fleet
Up towards the head, down towards the feet."

Long may the doctor honored be
Who let this saying fall!
He ought to have his effigy
By Phidias sculptured, so that he
May be discerned by all;
A monument forever thriving,
Boerhaave, Hippocrates, surviving!

REPROACH TO LAURA

Maiden, stay!—oh, whither wouldst thou go?
Do I still or pride or grandeur show?
Maiden, was it right?
Thou the giant mad'st a dwarf once more,
Scattered'st far the mountains that of yore
Climbed to glory's sunny height.

Thou hast doomed my flowerets to decay,
All the phantoms bright hast blown away,
Whose sweet follies formed the hero's trust;
All my plans that proudly raised their head
Thou dost, with gentle zephyr-tread,
Prostrate, laughing, in the dust.

To the godhead, eagle-like, I flew,—
Smiling, fortune's juggling wheel to view,
Careless wheresoe'er her ball might fly;
Hovering far beyond Cocytus' wave,
Death and life receiving like a slave—
Life and death from out one beaming eye!

Like the victors, who, with thunder-lance,
On the iron plain of glory dance,
Starting from their mistress' breast,—
From Aurora's rosy bed upsprings
God's bright sun, to roam o'er towns of kings,
And to make the young world blest!

35

Toward the hero doth this heart still strain?
Drink I, eagle, still the fiery rain
Of thine eye, that burneth to destroy?
In the glances that destructive gleam,
Laura's love I see with sweetness beam,—
Weep to see it—like a boy!

My repose, like yonder image bright,
Dancing in the waters—cloudless, light,
Maiden, hath been slain by thee!
On the dizzy height now totter I—
Laura—if from me—my Laura fly!
Oh, the thought to madness hurries me!

Gladly shout the revellers as they quaff,
Raptures in the leaf-crowned goblet laugh,
Jests within the golden wine have birth,
Since the maiden hath enslaved my mind,
I have left each youthful sport behind,
Friendless roam I o'er the earth.

Hear I still bright glory's thunder-tone?
Doth the laurel still allure me on?
Doth thy lyre, Apollo Cynthius?
In my breast no echoes now arise,
Every shamefaced muse in sorrow flies,—
And thou, too, Apollo Cynthius?

Shall I still be, as a woman, tame?
Do my pulses, at my country's name,
Proudly burst their prison-thralls?
Would I boast the eagle's soaring wing?
Do I long with Roman blood to spring,
When my Hermann calls?

Oh, how sweet the eye's wild gaze divine
Sweet to quaff the incense at that shrine!
Prouder, bolder, swells the breast.
That which once set every sense on fire,
That which once could every nerve inspire,
Scarce a half-smile now hath power to wrest!

That Orion might receive my fame,
On the time-flood's heaving waves my name
Rocked in glory in the mighty tide;
So that Kronos' dreaded scythe was shivered,
When against my monument is quivered,
Towering toward the firmament in pride.

Smil'st thou?—No? to me naught's perished now!
Star and laurel I'll to fools allow,
To the dead their marble cell;—
Love hath granted all as my reward,
High o'er man 'twere easy to have soared,
So I love him well!

THE SIMPLE PEASANT

MATTHEW.

Gossip, you'll like to hear, no doubt!
A learned work has just come out—
Messias is the name 'twill bear;
The man has travelled through the air,
And on the sun-beplastered roads
Has lost shoe-leather by whole loads,—
Has seen the heavens lie open wide,
And hell has traversed with whole hide.
The thought has just occurred to me
That one so skilled as he must be
May tell us how our flax and wheat arise.
What say you?—Shall I try to ascertain?

LUKE.

You fool, to think that any one so wise
About mere flax and corn would rack his brain.

ACTAEON

Thy wife is destined to deceive thee!
She'll seek another's arms and leave thee,
And horns upon thy head will shortly sprout!
How dreadful that when bathing thou shouldst see me
(No ether-bath can wash the stigma out),
And then, in perfect innocence, shouldst flee me!

MAN'S DIGNITY

I am a man!—Let every one
Who is a man, too, spring
With joy beneath God's shining sun,
And leap on high, and sing!

To God's own image fair on earth
Its stamp I've power to show;
Down to the front, where heaven has birth
With boldness I dare go.

'Tis well that I both dare and can!
When I a maiden see,
A voice exclaims: thou art a man!
I kiss her tenderly.

And redder then the maiden grows,
Her bodice seems too tight—
That I'm a man the maiden knows,
Her bodice therefore's tight.

Will she, perchance, for pity cry,
If unawares she's caught?
She finds that I'm a man—then, why
By her is pity sought?

I am a man; and if alone
She sees me drawing near,

I make the emperor's daughter run,
Though ragged I appear.

This golden watchword wins the smile
Of many a princess fair;
They call—ye'd best look out the while,
Ye gold-laced fellows there!

That I'm a man is fully shown
Whene'er my lyre I sweep;
It thunders out a glorious tone—
It otherwise would creep.

The spirit that my veins now hold,
My manhood calls its brother!
And both command, like lions bold,
And fondly greet each other.

From out this same creative flood
From which we men have birth,
Both godlike strength and genius bud,
And everything of worth.

My talisman all tyrants hates,
And strikes them to the ground;
Or guides us gladly through life's gates
To where the dead are found.

E'en Pompey, at Pharsalia's fight,
My talisman o'erthrew;
On German sand it hurled with might
Rome's sensual children, too.

Didst see the Roman, proud and stern,
Sitting on Afric's shore?
His eyes like Hecla seem to burn,
And fiery flames outpour.

Then comes a frank and merry knave,
And spreads it through the land:
"Tell them that thou on Carthage's grave
Hast seen great Marius stand!"

Thus speaks the son of Rome with pride,
Still mighty in his fall;
He is a man, and naught beside,—
Before him tremble all.

His grandsons afterwards began
Their portions to o'erthrow,
And thought it well that every man
Should learn with grace to crow.

For shame, for shame,—once more for shame!
The wretched ones?—they've even
Squandered the tokens of their fame,
The choicest gifts of heaven.

God's counterfeit has sinfully
Disgraced his form divine,
And in his vile humanity
Has wallowed like the swine.

The face of earth each vainly treads,
Like gourds, that boys in sport
Have hollowed out to human heads,
With skulls, whose brains are—naught.

Like wine that by a chemist's art
Is through retorts refined,
Their spirits to the deuce depart,
The phlegma's left behind.

From every woman's face they fly,
Its very aspect dread,—
And if they dared—and could not—why,
'Twere better they were dead.

They shun all worthies when they can,
Grief at their joy they prove—
The man who cannot make a man,
A man can never love!

The world I proudly wander o'er,
And plume myself and sing
I am a man!—Whoe'er is more?

Then leap on high, and spring!

THE MESSIAD

Religion 'twas produced this poem's fire;
Perverted also?—prithee, don't inquire!

THOUGHTS ON THE 1ST OCTOBER 1781

What mean the joyous sounds from yonder vine-clad height?
What the exulting Evoe? 63
Why glows the cheek? Whom is't that I, with pinions light,
Swinging the lofty Thyrsus see?

Is it the genius whom the gladsome throng obeys?
Do I his numerous train descry?
In plenty's teeming horn the gifts of heaven he sways,
And reels from very ecstacy!—

See how the golden grape in glorious beauty shines,
Kissed by the earliest morning-beams!
The shadow of yon bower, how lovingly it signs,
As it with countless blessings teams!

Ha! glad October, thou art welcome unto me!—
October's first-born, welcome thou!
Thanks of a purer kind, than all who worship thee,
More heartfelt thanks I'm bringing now!

For thou to me the one whom I have loved so well,
And love with fondness to the grave,
Who merits in my heart forevermore to dwell,—
The best of friends in Rieger 64 gave.

'Tis true thy breath doth rock the leaves upon the trees,
And sadly make their charms decay;

49

Gently they fall:—and swift, as morning phantasies
With those who waken, fly away.

'Tis true that on thy track the fleecy spoiler hastes,
Who makes all Nature's chords resound
With discord dull, and turns the plains and groves to wastes,
So that they sadly mourn around.

See how the gloomy forms of years, as on they roll,
Each joyous banquet overthrows,
When, in uplifted hand, from out the foaming bowl,
Joy's noble purple brightly flows!

See how they disappear, when friends sweet converse hold,
And loving wander arm-in-arm;
And, to revenge themselves on winter's north wind cold,
Upon each other's breasts grow warm!

And when spring's children smile upon us once again,
When all the youthful splendor bright,
When each melodious note of each sweet rapturous strain
Awakens with it each delight:

How joyous then the stream that our whole soul pervades!
What life from out our glances pours!
Sweet Philomela's song, resounding through the glades,
Ourselves, our youthful strength restores!

Oh, may this whisper breathe—(let Rieger bear in mind
The storm by which in age we're bent!)—
His guardian angel, when the evening's star so kind
Gleams softly from the firmament!

In silence be he led to yonder thundering height,
And guided be his eye, that he,
In valley and on plain, may see his friends aright.
And that, with growing ecstacy,

On yonder holy spot, when he their number tells,
He may experience friendship's bliss,
Now first unveiled, until with pride his bosom swells,
Conscious that all their love is his.

Then will the distant voice be loudly heard to say:
"And G—, too, is a friend of thine!
When silvery locks no more around his temples play,
G— still will be a friend of thine!"

"E'en yonder"—and now in his eye the crystal tear
Will gleam—"e'en yonder he will love!
Love thee too, when his heart, in yonder spring-like sphere,
Linked on to thine, can rapture prove!"

EPITAPH

Here lies a man cut off by fate
Too soon for all good men;
For sextons he died late—too late
For those who wield the pen.

QUIRL

You tell me that you feel surprise
Because Quirl's paper's grown in size;
And yet they're crying through the street
That there's a rise in bread and meat.

THE PLAGUE

A PHANTASY.

Plague's contagious murderous breath
God's strong might with terror reveals,
As through the dreary valley of death
With its brotherhood fell it steals!

Fearfully throbs the anguish-struck heart,
Horribly quivers each nerve in the frame;
Frenzy's wild laughs the torment proclaim,
Howling convulsions disclose the fierce smart.

Fierce delirium writhes upon the bed—
Poisonous mists hang o'er the cities dead;
Men all haggard, pale, and wan,
To the shadow-realm press on.
Death lies brooding in the humid air,
Plague, in dark graves, piles up treasures fair,
And its voice exultingly raises.
Funeral silence—churchyard calm,
Rapture change to dread alarm.—
Thus the plague God wildly praises!

MONUMENT OF MOOR THE ROBBER

'Tis ended!
Welcome! 'tis ended
Oh thou sinner majestic,
All thy terrible part is now played!

Noble abased one!
Thou, of thy race beginner and ender!
Wondrous son of her fearfulest humor,
Mother Nature's blunder sublime!

Through cloud-covered night a radiant gleam!
Hark how behind him the portals are closing!
Night's gloomy jaws veil him darkly in shade!
Nations are trembling,
At his destructive splendor afraid!
Thou art welcome! 'Tis ended!
Oh thou sinner majestic,
All thy terrible part is now played!

Crumble,—decay
In the cradle of wide-open heaven!
Terrible sight to each sinner that breathes,
When the hot thirst for glory
Raises its barriers over against the dread throne!
See! to eternity shame has consigned thee!
To the bright stars of fame
Thou hast clambered aloft, on the shoulders of shame!

Yet time will come when shame will crumble beneath thee,
When admiration at length will be thine!

With moist eye, by thy sepulchre dreaded,
Man has passed onward—
Rejoice in the tears that man sheddeth,
Oh thou soul of the judged!
With moist eye, by the sepulchre dreaded,
Lately a maiden passed onward,
Hearing the fearful announcement
Told of thy deeds by the herald of marble;
And the maiden—rejoice thee! rejoice thee!
Sought not to dry up her tears.
Far away I stood as the pearls were falling,
And I shouted: Amalia!

Oh, ye youths! Oh, ye youths!—
With the dangerous lightning of genius
Learn to play with more caution!
Wildly his bit champs the charger of Phoebus;
Though, 'neath the reins of his master,
More gently he rocks earth and heaven,
Reined by a child's hand, he kindles
Earth and heaven in blazing destruction!
Obstinate Phaeton perished,
Buried beneath the sad wreck.

Child of the heavenly genius!
Glowing bosom all panting for action!
Art thou charmed by the tale of my robber?
Glowing like time was his bosom, and panting for action!
He, like thee, was the child of the heavenly genius.
But thou smilest and goest—
Thy gaze flies through the realms of the world's long story,
Moor, the robber, it finds not there—
Stay, thou youth, and smile not!
Still survive all his sins and his shame—
Robber Moor liveth—in all but name.

THE BAD MONARCHS

Earthly gods—my lyre shall win your praise,
Though but wont its gentle sounds to raise
When the joyous feast the people throng;
Softly at your pompous-sounding names,
Shyly round your greatness purple flames,
Trembles now my song.

Answer! shall I strike the golden string,
When, borne on by exultation's wing,
O'er the battle-field your chariots trail?
When ye, from the iron grasp set free,
For your mistress' soft arms, joyously
Change your pond'rous mail?—

Shall my daring hymn, ye gods, resound,
While the golden splendor gleams around,
Where, by mystic darkness overcome,
With the thunderbolt your spleen may play,
Or in crime humanity array,
Till—the grave is dumb?

Say! shall peace 'neath crowns be now my theme?
Shall I boast, ye princes, that ye dream?—
While the worm the monarch's heart may tear,
Golden sleep twines round the Moor by stealth,
As he, at the palace, guards the wealth,
Guards—but covets ne'er.

Show how kings and galley-slaves, my Muse,
Lovingly one single pillow use,—
How their lightnings flatter, when surpressed,
When their humors have no power to harm,
When their mimic minotaurs are calm,
And—the lions rest!

Up, thou Hecate! with thy magic seal
Make the barred-up grave its wealth reveal,—
Hark! its doors like thunder open spring;
When death's dismal blast is heard to sigh,
And the hair on end stands fearfully,
Princes' bliss I sing!

Do I hear the strand, the coast, detect
Where your wishes' haughty fleet was wrecked,
Where was stayed your greatness' proud career
That they ne'er with glory may grow warm,
Night, with black and terror-spreading arm,
Forges monarchs here.

On the death-chest sadly gleams the crown,
With its heavy load of pearls weighed down,
And the sceptre, needed now no more.
In what splendor is the mould arrayed!
Yet but worms are with the body paid,
That—the world watched o'er.

Haughty plants within that humble bed
See how death their pomp decayed and fled
With unblushing ribaldry besets!
They who ruled o'er north and east and west
Suffer now his ev'ry nauseous jest,
And—no sultan threats?

Leap for joy, ye stubborn dumb, to-day,
And your heavy slumber shake away!
From the battle, victory upsprings!
Hearken to the trump's exulting song!
Ye are worshipped by the shouting throng!—
Rouse ye, then, ye kings!

Seven sleepers!—to the clarion hark!
How it rings, and how the fierce dogs bark!
Shouts from out a thousand barrels whizz;
Eager steeds are neighing for the wood,—
Soon the bristly boar rolls in his blood,—
Yours the triumph is!

But what now?—Are even princes dumb?
Tow'rd me scornful echoes ninefold come,
Stealing through the vault's terrific gloom—
Sleep assails the page by slow degrees,
And Madonna gives to you the keys
Of—her sleeping-room.

Not an answer—hushed and still is all—
Does the veil, then, e'en on monarchs fall,
Which enshrouds their humble flatt'rers glance?
And ye ask for worship in the dust,
Since the blind jade, Fate, a world has thrust
In your purse, perchance?

And ye clatter, giant puppet troops,
Marshalled in your proudly childish groups,
Like the juggler on the opera scene?—
Though the sound may please the vulgar ear,
Yet the skilful, filled with sadness, jeer
Powers so great, but mean.

Let your towering shame be hid from sight
In the garment of a sovereign's right,
From the ambush of the throne outspring!
Tremble, though, before the voice of song
Through the purple, vengeance will, ere long,
Strike down e'en a king!

THE SATYR AND MY MUSE

An aged satyr sought
Around my Muse to pass,
Attempting to pay court,
And eyed her fondly through his glass.

By Phoebus' golden torch,
By Luna's pallid light,
Around her temple's porch
Crept the unhappy sharp-eared wight;

And warbled many a lay,
Her beauty's praise to sing,
And fiercely scraped away
On his discordant fiddle-string.

With tears, too, swelled his eyes,
As large as nuts, or larger;
He gasped forth heavy sighs,
Like music from Silenus' charger.

The Muse sat still, and played
Within her grotto fair,
And peevishly surveyed
Signor Adonis Goatsfoot there.

"Who ever would kiss thee,
Thou ugly, dirty dunce?

Wouldst thou a gallant be,
As Midas was Apollo once?

"Speak out, old horned boor
What charms canst thou display?
Thou'rt swarthy as a Moor,
And shaggy as a beast of prey.

"I'm by a bard adored
In far Teutonia's land;
To him, who strikes the chord,
I'm linked in firm and loving band."

She spoke, and straightway fled
The spoiler,—he pursued her,
And, by his passion led,
Soon caught her, shouted, and thus wooed her:

"Thou prudish one, stay, stay!
And hearken unto me!
Thy poet, I dare say,
Repents the pledge he gave thee.

"Behold this pretty thing,—
No merit would I claim,—
Its weight I often fling
On many a clown's back, to his shame.

"His sharpness it increases,
And spices his discourse,
Instilling learned theses,
When mounted on his hobby-horse

"The best of songs are known,
Thanks to this heavy whip
Yet fool's blood 'tis alone
We see beneath its lashes drip.

"This lash, then, shall be his,
If thou'lt give me a smack;
Then thou mayest hasten, miss,
Upon thy German sweetheart's track."

The Muse, with purpose sly,
Ere long agreed to yield—
The satyr said good-by,
And now the lash I wield!

And I won't drop it here,
Believe in what I say!
The kisses of one's dear
One does not lightly throw away.

They kindle raptures sweet,
But fools ne'er know their flame!
The gentle Muse will kneel at honor's feet,
But cudgels those who mar her fame.

THE PEASANTS

Look outside, good friend, I pray!
Two whole mortal hours
Dogs and I've out here to-day
Waited, by the powers!

Rain comes down as from a spout,
Doomsday-storms rage round about,

Dripping are my hose;
Drenched are coat and mantle too,
Coat and mantle, both just new,
Wretched plight, heaven knows!
Pretty stir's abroad to-day;
Look outside, good friend, I pray!

Ay, the devil! look outside!
Out is blown my lamp,—
Gloom and night the heavens now hide,
Moon and stars decamp.
Stumbling over stock and stone,
Jerkin, coat, I've torn, ochone!

Let me pity beg
Hedges, bushes, all around,
Here a ditch, and there a mound,
Breaking arm and leg.
Gloom and night the heavens now hide

Ay, the devil! look outside!

Ay, the deuce, then look outside!
Listen to my prayer!
Praying, singing, I have tried,
Wouldst thou have me swear?
I shall be a steaming mass,
Freeze to rock and stone, alas!
If I don't remove.
All this, love, I owe to thee,
Winter-bumps thou'lt make for me,
Thou confounded love!
Cold and gloom spread far and wide!
Ay, the deuce! then look outside!

Thousand thunders! what's this now
From the window shoots?
Oh, thou witch! 'Tis dirt, I vow,
That my head salutes!
Rain, frost, hunger, tempests wild,
Bear I for the devil's child,
Now I'm vexed full sore.
Worse and worse 'tis! I'll begone.
Pray be quick, thou Evil One!
I'll remain no more.
Pretty tumult there's outside!
Fare thee well—I'll homeward stride.

THE WINTER NIGHT

Farewell! the beauteous sun is sinking fast,
The moon lifts up her head;
Farewell! mute night o'er earth's wide round at last
Her darksome raven-wing has spread.

Across the wintry plain no echoes float,
Save, from the rock's deep womb,
The murmuring streamlet, and the screech-owl's note,
Arising from the forest's gloom.

The fish repose within the watery deeps,
The snail draws in his head;
The dog beneath the table calmly sleeps,
My wife is slumbering in her bed.

A hearty welcome to ye, brethren mine!
Friends of my life's young spring!
Perchance around a flask of Rhenish wine
Ye're gathered now, in joyous ring.

The brimming goblet's bright and purple beams
Mirror the world with joy,
And pleasure from the golden grape-juice gleams—
Pleasure untainted by alloy.

Concealed behind departed years, your eyes
Find roses now alone;

And, as the summer tempest quickly flies,
Your heavy sorrows, too, are flown.

From childish sports, to e'en the doctor's hood,
The book of life ye thumb,
And reckon o'er, in light and joyous mood,
Your toils in the gymnasium;

Ye count the oaths that Terence—may he ne'er,
Though buried, calmly slumber!—
Caused you, despite Minelli's notes, to swear,—
Count your wry faces without number.

How, when the dread examinations came,
The boy with terror shook!
How, when the rector had pronounced his name,
The sweat streamed down upon his book!

All this is now involved in mist forever,
The boy is now a man,
And Frederick, wiser grown, discloses never
What little Fritz once loved to plan.

At length—a doctor one's declared to be,—
A regimental one!
And then,—and not too soon,—discover we
That plans soap-bubbles are alone. 68

Blow on! blow on! and let the bubbles rise,
If but this heart remain!
And if a German laurel as the prize
Of song, 'tis given me to gain!

THE WIRTEMBERGER

The name of Wirtemberg they hold
To come from Wirth am berg 69, I'm told.
A Wirtemberger who ne'er drinks
No Wirtemberger is, methinks!

THE MOLE

HUSBAND.
The boy's my very image! See!
Even the scars my small-pox left me!

WIFE.
I can believe it easily
They once of all my senses reft me.

HYMN TO THE ETERNAL

'Twixt the heavens and earth, high in the airy ocean,
In the tempest's cradle I'm borne with a rocking motion;
Clouds are towering,
Storms beneath me are lowering,
Giddily all the wonders I see,
And, O Eternal, I think of Thee!

All Thy terrible pomp, lend to the Finite now,
Mighty Nature! Oh, of Infinity, thou
Giant daughter!
Mirror God, as in water!
Tempest, oh, let thine organ-peal
God to the reasoning worm reveal!

Hark! it peals—how the rocks quiver beneath its growls
Zeboath's glorious name, wildly the hurricane howls!
Graving the while
With the lightning's style
"Creatures, do ye acknowledge me?"—
Spare us, Lord! We acknowledge Thee!

DIALOGUE

A.
Hark, neighbor, for one moment stay!
Herr Doctor Scalpel, so they say,
Has got off safe and sound;
At Paris I your uncle found
Fast to a horse's crupper bound,—
Yet Scalpel made a king his prey.

B.
Oh, dear me, no! A real misnomer!
The fact is, he has his diploma;
The other one has not.

A.
Eh? What? Has a diploma?
In Suabia may such things be got?

ON A CERTAIN PHYSIOGNOMIST

On every nose he rightly read
What intellects were in the head
And yet—that he was not the one
By whom God meant it to be done,
This on his own he never read.

TRUST IN IMMORTALITY

The dead has risen here, to live through endless ages;
This I with firmness trust and know.
I was first led to guess it by the sages,
The knaves convince me that 'tis really so.

APPENDIX OF POEMS ETC. IN SCHILLER'S DRAMATIC WORKS

The following variations appear in the first two verses of Hector's Farewell, as given in The Robbers, act ii. scene 2.

ANDROMACHE.
Wilt thou, Hector, leave me?—leave me weeping,
Where Achilles' murderous blade is heaping
Bloody offerings on Patroclus' grave?
Who, alas, will teach thine infant truly
Spears to hurl, the gods to honor duly,
When thou'rt buried 'neath dark Xanthus' wave?

HECTOR.
Dearest wife, go,—fetch my death-spear glancing,
Let me join the battle-dance entrancing,
For my shoulders bear the weight of Troy!
Heaven will be our Astyanax' protector!
Falling as his country's savior, Hector
Soon will greet thee in the realms of joy.

The following additional verse is found in Amalia's Song, as sung in The Robbers, act iii. scene 1. It is introduced between the first and second verses, as they appear in poems.
His embrace—what maddening rapture bound us!
Bosom throbbed 'gainst bosom with wild might;
Mouth and ear were chained—night reigned around us—

And the spirit winged toward heaven its flight.

From The Robbers, act iv. scene 5.

CHORUS OF ROBBERS.
What so good for banishing sorrow
As women, theft, and bloody affray?
We must dance in the air to-morrow,
Therefore let's be right merry to-day!

A free and jovial life we've led,
Ever since we began it.
Beneath the tree we make our bed,
We ply our task when the storm's o'erhead
And deem the moon our planet.
The fellow we swear by is Mercury,
A capital hand at our trade is he.

To-day we become the guests of a priest,
A rich farmer to-morrow must feed us;
And as for the future, we care not the least,
But leave it to heaven to heed us.

And when our throats with a vintage rare
We've long enough been supplying,
Fresh courage and strength we drink in there,
And with the evil one friendship swear,
Who down in hell is frying.

The groans o'er fathers reft of breath,
The sorrowing mothers' cry of death,
Deserted brides' sad sobs and tears.
Are sweetest music to our ears.

Ha! when under the axe each one quivering lies,
When they bellow like calves, and fall round us like flies,
Naught gives such pleasure to our sight,
It fills our ears with wild delight.
And when arrives the fatal day
The devil straight may fetch us!
Our fee we get without delay—
They instantly Jack-Ketch us.
One draught upon the road of liquor bright and clear,

And hip! hip! hip; hurrah! we're seen no longer here!

From The Robbers, act iv. scene 5.

EPITAPH

BRUTUS.
Ye are welcome, peaceful realms of light!
Oh, receive Rome's last-surviving son!
From Philippi, from the murderous fight,
Come I now, my race of sorrow run.—
Cassius, where art thou?—Rome overthrown!
All my brethren's loving band destroyed!
Safety find I at death's door alone,
And the world to Brutus is a void!

CAESAR.
Who now, with the ne'er-subdued-one's tread,
Hither from yon rocks makes haste to come?—
Ha! if by no vision I'm misled,
'Tis the footstep of a child of Rome.—
Son of Tiber—whence dost thou appear?
Stands the seven-hilled city as of yore
Oft her orphaned lot awakes my tear,
For alas, her Caesar is no more?

BRUTUS.
Ha! thou with the three-and-twenty wounds!
Who hath, dead one, summoned thee to light?
Back to gaping Orcus' fearful bonds,
Haughty mourner! triumph not to-night!
On Philippi's iron altar, lo!
Reeks now freedom's final victim's blood;
Rome o'er Brutus' bier feels her death-throe,—
He seeks Minos.—Back to thy dark flood!

CAESAR.
Oh, the death-stroke Brutus' sword then hurled!
Thou, too—Brutus—thou? Could this thing be?
Son! It was thy father!—Son! the world
Would have fallen heritage to thee!
Go—'mongst Romans thou art deemed immortal,
For thy steel hath pierced thy father's breast.

87

Go—and shout it even to yon portal:
"Brutus is 'mongst Romans deemed immortal,
For his steel hath pierced his father's breast."
Go—thou knowest now what on Lethe's strand
Made me a prisoner stand.—
Now, grim steersman, push thy bark from land!

BRUTUS.
Father, stay!—In all earth's realms so fair,
It hath been my lot to know but one,
Who with mighty Caesar could compare;
And of yore thou called'st him thy son.
None but Caesar could a Rome o'erthrow,
Brutus only made great Caesar fear;
Where lives Brutus, Caesar's blood must flow;
If thy path lies yonder, mine is here.

From Wallenstein's Camp, scene 1.
RECRUIT'S SONG

How sweet the wild sound
Of drum and of fife!
To roam o'er earth's round,
Lead a wandering life,
With steed trained aright,
And bold for the fight,
With a sword by the side,
To rove far and wide,—
Quick, nimble, and free
As the finch that we see
On bushes and trees,
Or braving the breeze,—
Huzza, then! the Friedlander's banner for me!

From Wallenstein's Camp, scene the last.

SECOND CUIRASSIER sings.

Up, up, my brave comrades! to horse! to horse!
Let us haste to the field and to freedom!
To the field, for 'tis there that is proved our hearts' force,
'Tis there that in earnest we need 'em!
None other can there our places supply,

Each must stand alone,—on himself must rely.

CHORUS.
None other can there our places supply,
Each must stand alone,—on himself must rely.

DRAGOON.
Now freedom appears from the world to have flown,
None but lords and their vassals one traces;
While falsehood and cunning are ruling alone
O'er the living cowardly races.
The man who can look upon death without fear—
The soldier,—is now the sole freeman left here.

CHORUS.
The man who can look upon death without fear—
The soldier,—is now the sole freeman left here.

FIRST YAGER.
The cares of this life, he casts them away,
Untroubled by fear or by sorrow;
He rides to his fate with a countenance gay,
And finds it to-day or to-morrow;
And if 'tis to-morrow, to-day we'll employ
To drink full deep of the goblet of joy,

CHORUS.
And if 'tis to-morrow, to-day we'll employ
To drink full deep of the goblet of joy.
[They refill their glasses and drink.

CAVALRY SERGEANT.
The skies o'er him shower his lot filled with mirth,
He gains, without toil, its full measure;
The peasant, who grubs in the womb of the earth,
Believes that he'll find there the treasure,
Through lifetime he shovels and digs like a slave,
And digs—till at length he has dug his own grave.

CHORUS.
Through lifetime he shovels and digs like a slave,
And digs—till at length he has dug his own grave.

FIRST YAGER.
The horseman, as well as his swift-footed beast,
Are guests by whom all are affrighted,
When glimmer the lamps at the wedding feast,
In the banquet he joins uninvited;
He woos not long, and with gold he ne'er buys,
But carries by storm love's blissful prize.

CHORUS.
He woos not long, and with gold he ne'er buys,
But carries by storm love's blissful prize.

SECOND CUIRASSIER.
Why weeps the maiden? Why sorrows she so?
Let me hence, let me hence, girl, I pray thee?
The soldier on earth no sure quarters can know,
With true love he ne'er can repay thee.
Fate hurries him onward with fury blind,
His peace he never can leave behind.

CHORUS.
Fate hurries him onward with fury blind,
His peace he can never leave behind,

FIRST YAGER.
(Taking his two neighbors by the hand. The rest do the same,
forming a large semi-circle.)
Away, then, my comrades, our chargers let's mount!
In the battle the bosom bounds lightly!
Youth boils, and life's goblet still foams at the fount,
Away! while the spirit glows brightly!
Unless ye have courage your life to stake,
That life ye never your own can make!

CHORUS.
Unless ye have courage your life to stake,
That life ye never your own can make!

From William Tell, act i. scene 1.

SCENE—The high rocky shore of the Lake of Lucerne, opposite Schwytz.

The lake forms an inlet in the land; a cottage is near the shore; a fisher-boy

90

is rowing in a boat. Beyond the lake are seen the green pastures, the village. and farms of Schwytz glowing in the sunshine. On the left of the spectator are the peaks of the Hacken, enveloped in clouds; on his right, in the distance, are seen the glaciers. Before the curtain rises the RANZ DES VACHES, and the musical sound of the cattle-bells are heard, and continue also for some time after the scene opens.

FISHER-BOY (sings in his boat).
AIR—Ranz des Vaches.

Bright smiles the lake, as it woos to its deep,—
A boy on its margin of green lies asleep;
Then hears he a strain,
Like the flute's gentle note,
Sweet as voices of angels
In Eden that float.
And when he awakens, with ecstasy blest,
The waters are playing all over his breast,
From the depths calls a voice
"Dearest child, with me go!
I lure down the sleeper,
I draw him below."

HERDSMAN (on the mountain).
AIR—Variation of the Ranz des Vaches.

Ye meadows, farewell!
Ye pastures so glowing!
The herdsman is going,
For summer has fled!
We depart to the mountain; we'll come back again,
When the cuckoo is calling,—when wakens the strain,—
When the earth is tricked out with her flowers so gay,
When the stream sparkles bright in the sweet month of May.
Ye meadows, farewell!
Ye pastures so glowing!
The herdsman is going,
For summer has fled!

CHAMOIS-HUNTER (appearing on the top of a rock).
AIR—Second Variation of the Ranz des Vaches.

O'er the heights growls the thunder, while quivers the bridge,

91

Yet no fear feels the hunter, though dizzy the ridge;
He strides on undaunted,
O'er plains icy-bound,
Where spring never blossoms,
Nor verdure is found;

And, a broad sea of mist lying under his feet,
Man's dwellings his vision no longer can greet;

The world he but views
When the clouds broken are—
With its pastures so green,
Through the vapor afar.

From William Tell, act iii. scene 1.

WALTER sings.

Bow and arrow bearing,
Over hills and streams
Moves the hunter daring,
Soon as daylight gleams.

As all flying creatures
Own the eagle's sway,
So the hunter, Nature's
Mounts and crags obey.

Over space he reigneth,
And he makes his prize
All his bolt attaineth,
All that creeps or flies.

From William Tell, act iv. scene 3.

CHORUS OF BROTHERS OF MERCY.

Death comes to man with hasty stride,
No respite is to him e'er given;
He's stricken down in manhood's pride,
E'en in mid race from earth he's driven.
Prepared, or not, to go from here,
Before his Judge he must appear!

From Turandot, act ii. scene 4.

RIDDLE.

The tree whereon decay
All those from mortals sprung,—
Full old, and yet whose spray
Is ever green and young;
To catch the light, it rolls
Each leaf upon one side;
The other, black as coals,
The sun has ne'er descried.

It places on new rings
As often as it blows;
The age, too, of all things
To mortal gaze it shows.
Upon its bark so green
A name oft meets the eye,
Yet 'tis no longer seen,
When it grows old and dry.
This tree—what can it mean?
I wait for thy reply. 70

From Mary Stuart, act iii, scene 1.

SCENE—A Park. MARY advances hastily from behind some trees.
HANNAH KENNEDY follows her slowly.

MARY.

Let me my newly-won liberty taste!
Let me rejoice as a child once again!
And, as on pinions, with airy foot hast
Over the tapestried green of the plain!
Have I escaped from my prison so drear?
Shall I no more in my sad dungeon pine?
Let me in long and in thirsty draughts here
Drink in the breezes, so free, so divine

Thanks, thanks, ye trees, in smiling verdure dressed,
In that ye veil my prison-walls from sight!

I'll dream that I am free and blest
Why should I waken from a dream so bright?
Do not the spacious heavens encompass me?
Behold! my gaze, unshackled, free,
Pierces with joy the trackless realms of light!
There, where the gray-tinged hills of mist project,
My kingdom's boundaries begin;
Yon clouds, that tow'rd the south their course direct,
France's far-distant ocean seek to win.

Swiftly-flying clouds, hardy sailors through air!
Mortal hath roamed with ye, sailed with ye, ne'er!
Greetings of love to my youthful home bear!
I am a prisoner, I am in chains,
Ah, not a herald, save ye, now remains,
Free through the air hath your path ever been,
Ye are not subject to England's proud queen!

Yonder's a fisherman trimming his boat.
E'en that frail skiff from all danger might tear me,
And to the dwellings of friends it might bear me.
Scarcely his earnings can keep life afloat.
Richly with treasures his lap I'd heap over,—
Oh! what a draught should reward him to-day!
Fortune held fast in his nets he'd discover,
If in his bark he would take me away!

Hear'st thou the horn of the hunter resound,
Wakening the echo through forest and plain?
Ah, on my spirited courser to bound!
Once more to join in the mirth-stirring train!
Hark! how the dearly-loved tones come again!
Blissful, yet sad, the remembrance they wake;
Oft have they fallen with joy on mine ear,
When in the highlands the bugle rang clear,
Rousing the chase over mountain and brake.

From The Maid of Orleans, Prologue, scene 4.

JOAN OF ARC (soliloquizing).

Farewell, ye mountains, and ye pastures dear,
Ye still and happy valleys, fare ye well!

No longer may Joan's footsteps linger here,
Joan bids ye now a long, a last farewell!

Ye meadows that I watered, and each bush
Set by my hands, ne'er may your verdure fail!
Farewell, ye grots, ye springs that cooling gush
Thou echo, blissful voice of this sweet vale,
So wont to give me back an answering strain,—
Joan must depart, and ne'er return again!

Ye haunts of all my silent joys of old,
I leave ye now behind forevermore!
Disperse, ye lambs, far o'er the trackless wold!
She now hath gone who tended you of yore!
I must away to guard another fold,
On yonder field of danger, stained with gore.
Thus am I bidden by a spirit's tone
'Tis no vain earthly longing drives me on.

For He who erst to Moses on the height
Of Horeb, in the fiery bush came down,
And bade him stand in haughty Pharaoh's sight,
He who made choice of Jesse's pious son,
The shepherd, as his champion in the fight,—
He who to shepherds grace hath ever shown,
He thus addressed me from this lofty tree:
"Go hence! On earth my witness thou shalt be!

"In rugged brass, then, clothe thy members now,
In steel thy gentle bosom must be dressed!
No mortal love thy heart must e'er allow,
With earthly passion's sinful flame possessed.
Ne'er will the bridal wreath adorn thy brow,
No darling infant blossom on thy breast;
Yet thou with warlike honors shalt be laden,
Raising thee high above each earthly maiden.

"For when the bravest in the fight despair,
When France appears to wait her final blow,
Then thou my holy oriflamme must bear;
And, as the ripened corn the reapers mow,
Hew down the conqueror as he triumphs there;
His fortune's wheel thou thus wilt overthrow,

95

To France's hero-sons salvation bring,
Deliver Rheims once more, and crown thy king!"

The Lord hath promised to send down a sign
A helmet he hath sent, it comes from Him,—
His sword endows mine arm with strength divine,
I feel the courage of the cherubim;
To join the battle-turmoil how I pine!
A raging tempest thrills through every limb;
The summons to the field bursts on mine ear,
My charger paws the ground, the trump rings clear.

From The Maid of Orleans, act iv. scene 1.

SCENE—A hall prepared for a festival. The pillars are covered with festoons of flowers; flutes and hautboys are heard behind the scene.

JOAN OF ARC (soliloquizing).

Each weapon rests, war's tumults cease to sound,
While dance and song succeed the bloody fray;
Through every street the merry footsteps bound,
Altar and church are clad in bright array,
And gates of branches green arise around,
Over the columns twine the garlands gay;
Rheims cannot hold the ever-swelling train
That seeks the nation-festival to gain.

All with one joyous feeling are elate,
One single thought is thrilling every breast;
What, until now, was severed by fierce hate,
Is by the general rapture truly blessed.
By each who called this land his parent-state,
The name of Frenchman proudly is confessed;
The glory is revived of olden days,
And to her regal son France homage pays.

Yet I who have achieved this work of pride,
I cannot share the rapture felt by all:
My heart is changed, my heart is turned aside,
It shuns the splendor of this festival;
'Tis in the British camp it seeks to hide,—
'Tis on the foe my yearning glances fall;

And from the joyous circle I must steal,
My bosom's crime o'erpowering to conceal.

Who? I? What! in my bosom chaste
Can mortal's image have a seat?
This heart, by heavenly glory graced,—
Dares it with earthly love to beat?
The saviour of my country, I,—
The champion of the Lord Most High,
Own for my country's foe a flame—
To the chaste sun my guilt proclaim,
And not be crushed beneath my shame?

(The music behind the scene changes into a soft, melting melody.)

Woe! oh woe! what strains enthralling!
How bewildering to mine ear
Each his voice beloved recalling,
Charming up his image dear!

Would that battle-tempests bound me!
Would that spears were whizzing round me
In the hotly-raging strife!
Could my courage find fresh life!

How those tones, those voices blest
Coil around my bosom burning
All the strength within my breast
Melting into tender yearning,
Into tears of sadness turning!

(The flutes are again heard—she falls into a silent melancholy.)

Gentle crook! oh that I never
For the sword had bartered thee!
Sacred oak! why didst thou ever
From thy branches speak to me?
Would that thou to me in splendor,
Queen of heaven, hadst ne'er come down!
Take—all claim I must surrender,—
Take, oh take away thy crown!

Ah, I open saw yon heaven,

Saw the features of the blest!
Yet to earth my hopes are riven,
In the skies they ne'er can rest!
Wherefore make me ply with ardor
This vocation, terror-fraught?
Would this heart were rendered harder.
That by heaven to feel was taught!

To proclaim Thy might sublime
Those select, who, free from crime,
In Thy lasting mansions stand;
Send Thou forth Thy spirit-band,
The immortal, and the pure,
Feelingless, from tears secure
Never choose a maiden fair,
Shepherdess' weak spirit ne'er!

Kings' dissensions wherefore dread I,
Why the fortune of the fight?
Guilelessly my lambs once fed I
On the silent mountain-height.
Yet Thou into life didst bear me,
To the halls where monarchs throne.
In the toils of guilt to snare me—
Ah, the choice was not mine own!

FOOTNOTES

62A pointless satire upon Klopstock and his Messias.
63Schiller, who is not very particular about the quantities of
classical names, gives this word with the o long—which is, of course,
the correct quantity—in The Gods of Greece.
64A well-known general, who died in 1783.
65See the play of The Robbers.
66Written in consequence of the ill-treatment Schiller experienced
at the hands of the Grand Duke Charles of Wirtemberg.
67Written in the Suabian dialect.
68An allusion to the appointment of regimental surgeon, conferred
upon Schiller by the Grand Duke Charles in 1780, when he was twenty-one
years of age.
69The Landlord on the Mountain.
70The year.

FRIEDRICH SCHILLER

Made in the USA
Middletown, DE
05 October 2022

12048114R00056